The Torn Heart

By
Ruth Bawell

Table of Contents

Unsolicited Testimonials............... 4
FREE GIFT.............................. 5
CHAPTER ONE............................ 6
CHAPTER TWO........................... 14
CHAPTER THREE......................... 24
CHAPTER FOUR.......................... 40
CHAPTER FIVE.......................... 48
CHAPTER SIX........................... 53
FREE GIFT............................. 62
Please Check out My Other Works...... 63
Thank You............................. 64

Unsolicited Testimonials

By **Phyllis**

★★★★★ Love Ruth!

I love Ruth's books! Her mysteries are the best!

★★★★★ Love This Author

Ruth Bawell is very creative and a great writer! All her books have left me unable to stop reading till the ending! There were a few Amish fact mistakes, like unmarried man having a beard, but the plot was so good I overlooked that!

By **Steve M**

★★★★★ I love romance stories August 5, 2017
I love romance stories... well written with her usual twists to the story still enjoyed them very much Once I start I can't put it down.

By **Bones**

★★★★★ Amish County Stories
I love all the Amish County stories! Each one brings so much excitement! Ruth Bawell is also a wonderful writer!

By **Kindle Customer**

★★★★★ Good clean writing.
The Amish stories of Ruth Bawell are authentic, faith-filled writings. They are short, more the length of novellas or longer short stories. Always clean, always uplifting.

FREE GIFT

Just to say thanks for checking our works we like to gift you

Our Exclusive Never Before Released Books

100% FREE!

Please GO TO

http://cleanromancepublishing.com/gift

And get your FREE gift

Thanks for being such a wonderful client.

CHAPTER ONE

"Just one more patch and this quilt is complete," Candace Shrock said, holding up the quilt for the other young women in the room to see.

"It's exquisite!" Rebecca Miller exclaimed.

"I'm truly pleased with how it has turned out," Candace replied, as compliments were heaped upon her work.

"You're so talented, Candace," Rebecca said.

"Well, so are you all," Candace replied. "And that's why it's so wonderful that we can all spend time here in this barn quilting together."

"Well," a dark-haired girl, Lydia Bieler, said, "we are grateful for the use of your barn. It was mighty good of your daed and mamm to let you use it exclusively to make and store your quilts."

"It's our exclusive Quilting Barn," Candace smiled back. "And it's such a joy to spend time together with you all doing what we love and creating such beautiful works of art." She sighed. "And soon we will have enough quilts to display and invite people here to view and buy them."

"Let's give the barn a name," Rebecca suggested. "Something intriguing that will attract buyers to come here."

"I think *The Quilting Barn* is a fine enough name," Lydia said. "And it tells people exactly what it is too."

"You're right," Candace replied. "The Quilting Barn it is."

"We can get someone to make us a really nice signboard," Rebecca said.

And so the group of young women chatted, laughed, dreamed, planned, and quilted.

Some days later, Candace rose earlier than usual, eager to put in some work on a quilt she had designed for a bride-to-be. She lit her lantern and glanced at the clock in the kitchen as she did so. She would have at least an hour, she gauged, to put in a few patches.

The winter air was biting cold, and Candace shivered in her gown and cloak. The snow crunched under her sturdy shoes as she made her way to the barn in the semi-darkness.

As she reached the barn, however, she stopped and cocked her head to one side. There was a sound, almost but not entirely, like a pig grunting… or was it the snort of a horse? Had a pig or a horse wandered into the barn, and if so, how? Had she left the door open the previous day?

Candace opened the barn door gingerly, holding her lantern aloft and looking in at the shadows that danced on the floors and the walls around her. Suddenly, she jumped as a strange sound assailed her ears. She ran back, her heart thumping, wondering if there was an intruder there or a frightened animal, and then retraced her steps slowly, still holding her lantern up to light the path ahead of her.

"Who's there?" she called, instantly feeling silly for calling out to what could only be some wild creature that had wandered in from the surrounding woods.

She changed her approach and used a variety of animal calls instead, mostly to bolster her own failing courage.

"Candace?" she heard Ruby, her mother, call out from the house. "Is that you, dear? What's wrong? Did one of the animals get out or go missing?"

"*Mamm*!" Candace called back in relief. "Could you come out here, please? I'm not sure what's wrong, but I heard sounds from the barn."

"Hold on, dear, I'm coming!" Ruby said.

The two women inched forward slowly, each more apprehensive than the other as to what lay within the barn that hadn't been there when Candace closed the doors the previous evening.

"You really should consider locking the doors, dear," Ruby murmured.

"This is our home and it should be safe," Candace replied in a hoarse whisper.

"Now, let's go inside together," Ruby said. "It's bound to be an animal, so be careful, because a frightened horse can be dangerous."

"It sounded more like a pig," Candace said, "but I can't be sure."

Carefully, they stepped inside the barn.

"Oh no!" Candace exclaimed as her lantern light filled the space.

"Who did this?" Ruby said, her hand flying to her mouth.

"*Mamm*, could you hold my lantern, please?" Candace asked, and rushed forward, her voice breaking on a sob.

"My beautiful quilts! Oh, my beautiful quilts!" she cried.

"Are they damaged?" Ruby asked, drawing closer, holding her lantern and Candace's up together, to shed more light on the scene before them.

The finished quilts that had been neatly folded and laid out in a large closet on the side of the barn were now on the floor, and some of the cushioning material used to line the quilts had been rolled up and flung aside.

Ruby drew in her breath in shock. "They're… muddy… Oh, Candace, this is awful."

Candace stood there in shock, sobbing. "*Mamm*," she said, "oh *Mamm*, who could have done this?"

"A thief, perhaps," Ruby replied, picking the muddied quilts off the floor. "Obviously, an animal couldn't have taken all these out of the closet." She piled the quilts on a table and turned to her daughter.

"Stay right here, child," she said. "I'll go inside and fetch a lock."

"But the damage is done," Candace wept.

"And we want to make sure that no further harm comes to those beautiful quilts," Ruby replied. "Now, don't you worry, we will find a way to restore them to their former beauty."

Candace couldn't prevent a fresh flood of tears at the word '*former,*' and Ruby felt helpless.

"Don't cry, Candace," Ruby consoled her. "We will find out who is responsible for all of this."

"I am," they heard a voice say, and both the women sprang back as a fair-haired young man came into view, adjusting a hat on his head. He looked disheveled, and though his attire was Amish, he was obviously not from their village.

"Who are you?" Ruby asked, stepping forward even as she shielded Candace with a protective right arm.

"Caleb Raber," the man said, tipping his hat.

"You're not from Crescent Creek Village, are you?" Ruby asked.

"No, ma'am, I am not. I am, in fact, bound for Fair View Village," Caleb Raber replied.

"What do you have against us that you would come into our barn and ruin my quilts?" Candace asked tearfully.

Caleb looked contrite. "My apologies," he murmured. "I am truly, truly sorry. I got off the bus on the way to Fair View in order to get a cup of hot chocolate, and the bus took off without me. I trudged on for miles in the snow, frozen to the bones, and stumbled upon your barn where I took refuge for the night."

"So those were your snores that I heard?" Candace queried. "I thought they were animal sounds."

"I was so weary," Caleb replied. "I didn't wake until I heard your voices."

"You could have knocked on our door," Ruby said, "and you would have received shelter and a meal, instead of which you have wreaked havoc here."

"I meant no harm," Caleb replied.

"But you inflicted great harm," Candace shot back. "And that is unkind and unfair." She ran to the table where Ruby had piled the quilts. "These quilts are ruined—some of them anyway, and each of them takes so many weeks to complete. How could you do this?"

"I was desperate," Caleb said helplessly, looking away. "And cold."

"And like my *mamm* said, you could have knocked on our door, and we would have offered you shelter and a hot meal," Candace cried. "Rather than doing what you did!"

"But because we do as our Lord directs," Ruby said, "we will still offer you lodging and a meal. So come inside and warm up by the fire, and I will give you something to eat."

"But *Mamm*!" Candace cried. "My quilts!"

"My dear child," Ruby murmured, "we must never turn away someone who is cold and hungry. Never."

"I give you my word," Caleb said, "to do whatever I can to restore your quilts to their former beauty."

"*Former*!" Candace cried, her voice catching on a sob. "*Former*! That's the word my *mamm* used only minutes ago. And now you too! Is this a judgment on me for some wrong I have done? That all my labor has come to naught?"

"Candace, my dear child," Ruby said in a soothing voice. "I know your quilts have been spoiled, but you must not be dramatic. This is not the time for that. Let us concentrate on giving our guest a roof over his head and some food to warm his belly."

"Oh my!" Candace exclaimed hotly. Her face had turned a vivid shade of red discernible even in the lamplight as her eyes flashed with righteous anger. Then, she turned and stomped out of the barn.

CHAPTER TWO

"Please forgive me," Caleb said later, his eyes fixed anxiously on Candace.

"You've asked forgiveness already, son, and it has been given to you," Ruby replied.

"Has it?" Candace muttered as she set a dish of scrambled eggs on the kitchen table.

"The Lord forgave us our trespasses so that we could forgive them that trespass against us, remember, Candace?" Ruby scolded gently.

"I created something beautiful that somebody ruined, though I did nothing to deserve such treatment!" Candace said.

"And I am truly sorry," Caleb declared emphatically.

"God created a beautiful world for us to enjoy, and everyone did everything they possibly could to tarnish that beauty, didn't they, Candace?" Ruby declared quietly. "But yet He forgave us. Shouldn't we also extend that same forgiveness to others?"

"The wound is fresh," Candace murmured, slicing a loaf of bread and setting it on the table.

"Come, Caleb Raber," Ruby said. "Eat some breakfast, and then I will show you your room and where you can wash and change."

"I have a bag with my clothes in your barn," Caleb said sheepishly.

"You may fetch it after you eat, and then you can freshen up and get some rest," Ruby replied.

"Please, ma'am…" Caleb began.

"You may call me Miss Ruby. And this is my daughter Candace," Ruby said. "She's our youngest, and all her older siblings are married and away. But my husband, Amos, will join us shortly."

"Please… Miss Ruby," Caleb said, "I would like to help with chores or anything else that you would like me to do… while I'm here."

"And approximately how long do you intend on staying?" Candace queried coldly. "Your village, Fair View, isn't that far from here, and I'm sure you can be on your way by midday so as not to delay your arrival and cause anxiety to the ones waiting for you."

Caleb looked down at his plate, closing his eyes while Ruby prayed over the food. The scrambled eggs looked appetizing, and as he opened his eyes, he saw Candace set a plate of fried bacon on the table. The aroma made him realize just how hungry he was, and he fell on his food with the air of a man who has been starved for weeks.

"I could leave right after breakfast," he said, "but I would like to restore your quilts to their umm… rightful state… before I leave. So I beg you, good people, to please let me stay just a day or two more with you."

He looked up to see Candace's eyes upon him. They were cold and distant and still carried the hurt she felt at seeing her beautiful quilts sullied.

"Would that be alright?" he asked.

"Your staying a few more days?" Ruby asked. "Of course. You are our guest, and you seem eager to make reparation for the mistake that you have made. So please… stay, and if you restore the quilts, it would no doubt take a load off Candace's mind. She means to turn her love for quilting into a business venture, you see."

"Oh," Caleb murmured. "I could help. I am good at these things—getting small enterprises off the ground."

"I can see how you would consider this to be *small*," Candace retorted. "But for me, it is a *big* venture, and I wouldn't want to take any risks with it."

"I didn't mean it that way," Caleb said hurriedly, thinking regretfully that he had forever incurred the wrath of Candace and that nothing could ever absolve him of his mistake.

He stole a look at her again. Under less hostile circumstances, he might have felt some interest in this girl with the flashing eyes. He hadn't intended to ruin her works of art. He had rummaged in the closet for something to form a bed for his weary, freezing body and had fallen on the quilts with joy. In the darkness of the barn, he had not realized that they were brand-new and unused. Instead, he had been so grateful to feel their warmth and had thought they were perhaps rejected bedclothes consigned to the barn, perhaps to give to the poor during Christmas time.

Even now, he had not yet quite determined what the fuss was all about, having got but the barest glimpse of one quilt in the lantern light. He knew very little about quilting, but he knew something about starting up a business and getting it going. Perhaps he could advise her as he had advised his mother about her baking business.

Caleb cringed inwardly at the memory. It was his desire to help with her business that had got him into trouble in the first place. It was, in fact, the very reason why he was here.

"I will take care of the damage to the quilts myself," Candace declared. "I think I am well able to do so." She pinned Caleb down with her vivid blue eyes. "As I said before, I don't want to keep you from your family, especially as you might be traveling back home to spend some time with them."

Caleb cleared his throat. "Of course. I want nothing more than to do as you ask," he said. Even as he spoke, he glanced out of the window, and his spirits soared. "It's snowing, you see, so perhaps it wouldn't be the best thing for me to consider resuming my journey home at this point. Maybe later. Tomorrow perhaps. Or the day after."

Ruby followed Caleb's eyes to the window, and she left the table to look outside. "Oh dear," she sighed. "It's snowing. Now what will become of all the winter activities that we have planned?"

"Postpone them for a few days," Caleb suggested. "I would be happy to help you with them, of course."

"You mustn't think of leaving today, Caleb," Ruby said. "In fact, I think you should stay on until the snow stops. It just wouldn't be safe for you to venture out in this weather." She heard the kitchen door open and smiled broadly. "Here's Amos now."

"*Gute mariye, Daed*," Candace greeted her father.

"And who is this?" Amos asked, stepping into the kitchen and shaking the snow off his coat.

"This is our guest, Caleb Raber," Ruby replied.

"I'm more of a trespasser, actually," Caleb declared, standing up and shrugging his shoulders.

"How so?" Amos asked, sitting down at the table and helping himself to some bacon and eggs.

"Caleb has had a bit of an adventure," Ruby explained. "While traveling to Fair View Village, he left his bus for a mug of hot chocolate, and the bus left him behind. He trudged through the snow and came upon our barn and took shelter there."

"I'm afraid I also used what I assumed were quilts that had been discarded, because they were stored in the barn, and in the process may have spoiled one or two with mud stains," Caleb added.

"*May* have?" Candace murmured audibly.

"Well… I did," Caleb replied. "And I have just apologized and told Miss Ruby and Candace that I would very much like to clean the quilts and make them as good as new."

"That's very honorable of you," Amos remarked.

"Oh, it's the least I can do," Caleb answered, stealing another look at Candace, who appeared to be about to erupt.

"It's snowing," Amos said to Caleb, "and it's coming down very hard. You must stay until the storm passes."

"I am very grateful for your hospitality," Caleb replied.

"Hopefully, the snow will clear soon," Candace remarked, "and then you can resume your journey. As I mentioned earlier, Fair View isn't that far away. In fact, I'm sure *Daed* could drop you there in our buggy."

Amos nodded. "Of course I can. And I would be happy too just as soon as this snow stops," he said. "In the meantime, please make yourself comfortable, Caleb, and let us know if there's anything that you need."

"The only thing that I need is the opportunity to make up for the damage that I inadvertently caused," Caleb said.

"Come with me," Amos said after breakfast, "and you can help chop some wood. We will need to keep stoking the fire so that we all don't freeze to death."

Caleb followed Amos, glad that he could do something... anything... to pay for his stay. He chopped wood and groomed the horses, helped Amos clean the pigsty, and then helped Ruby get the chickens into the chicken coop's warmest part. When he spied Candace setting off for the barn, he quickly followed her, determined to help her in any way that he could.

"The roof appears to have sprung a leak," Caleb remarked, looking up at the ceiling of the barn.

"It wasn't there yesterday, so I wonder, did you have something to do with it?" Candace asked.

Caleb flushed. "No. And again, I'm sorry about the quilts. I can repair the roof for you."

"You don't have to," Candace said. "We can wait for better weather and have members of our community over to help with the repairs."

"You might need to do something immediately," Caleb said, pointing out a section of the roof where melted snow was now beginning to drip inside. "Obviously, the weight of the snow on the roof is causing some trouble, and I can fix that."

Candace said nothing. She merely began to stack the quilts in the closet.

"I've never seen a barn with such an elaborate closet," Caleb remarked.

"That ought to have tipped you off about the value of these quilts," Candace said. "Oh dear!" she exclaimed, clapping her hand over her mouth and stepping away from the closet.

"What is it?" Caleb asked, coming to stand beside her and looking inside the closet at a rapidly expanding damp patch.

"How did this happen?" Candace queried, shaking her head from side to side.

"Because the back of your closet is the wall of the barn, and obviously, there's some damp seeping through," Caleb replied. "I can fix all of this. Just give me some time," he added.

"Where do I store these quilts in the meantime?" Candace said, almost to herself.

"I see a very sturdy chest there," Caleb said, pointing to a large vintage chest that had belonged to Candace's grandmother. "Perhaps you could store them there."

"Don't you think I would have if I could?" Candace retorted. "That chest isn't as sturdy as it looks, and it's not the right place for these quilts."

Caleb sighed. "Then give the quilts to me, and I will carry them indoors where you can store them safely." He grinned. "Isn't it a good thing I took them out of the closet and umm… slept on top of them? Ironically, that helped save most of them."

"I can't believe you are making light of a very serious situation," Candace shot back. "And thank you, but I will take the quilts indoors myself."

CHAPTER THREE

"Who's that?" Rebecca asked, looking out of the living room window. They were seated around a coffee table, quilting and sipping mugs of hot chocolate in between.

"That's Caleb Raber, the person who ruined some of the quilts," Candace said, rolling her eyes.

"He is handsome," Lydia observed. "How old is he? Is he married?"

"He is twenty-two and not married," Candace replied. "But why are you asking?"

"Candace, you are twenty and single, and haven't met anyone in our village who looks even remotely like Caleb Raber," Lydia giggled.

"He ruined my quilts," Candace said. "And anyway, I'm not interested."

"Where are the ruined quilts anyway?" Rebecca asked.

"Caleb said he was going to restore them to their former beauty," Candace said. "And he also said he was going to repair the barn roof, which is why he has been in there these past few days."

"Have you taken a look inside?" Lydia asked.

Candace shook her head. "I couldn't bear to," she answered. "The beautiful closet that *Daed* put in for me is now barely usable, and the snow is melting through the roof and forming patches on the wall. Such a tragedy."

"Oh Candace, have some faith in the young man's abilities," Lydia said. "I'm sure that Caleb will work wonders on the barn. He seems the sort of person who could."

"You haven't even met him yet," Candace observed. "You've only seen him from a distance."

"*Gute mariye*," a voice greeted them from the doorway. "I'm sorry to intrude, but..."

"Caleb!" Candace exclaimed. "What are you doing here?"

"I'm sorry, I just wanted to bring you these," Caleb replied.

"Oh my!" Lydia exclaimed, looking at the quilts that Caleb was laying out on the back of a sofa to display his handiwork.

"You've got the stains out!" Candace breathed, almost reverently.

"I most certainly have," Caleb replied. "As I believed I would."

"I told you to have faith in his abilities," Lydia said.

"You did?" Caleb smiled.

"She did," Rebecca nodded. "And she was right."

Candace was running her hands over the quilts. "How did you manage to get the stains out?" she queried.

"I used a family recipe," Caleb replied. "I never realized that it would come in so handy one day." He looked appealingly at Candace. "So, am I forgiven?"

"Of course you are," Lydia replied on Candace's behalf. "Isn't he, Candace?"

"I suppose you are," Candace murmured, her eyes never leaving the quilts. "These look as good as new!"

"I'm Caleb Raber," Caleb introduced himself to Lydia and Rebecca.

"This is Lydia, and that is Rebecca," Candace said hurriedly. "They are my friends and quilting partners." She looked at him. "And I'm sorry for being so upset over the quilts. Thank you for restoring them. I am so grateful."

"How long are you staying here in Crescent Creek?" Lydia asked Caleb.

Caleb shrugged. "Well, there is the barn to repair, so that might take a few days, and then I will have to leave for Fair View," he replied.

"If you need help repairing the barn, I can ask my fiancé, David, to come over whenever you need him to," Lydia offered.

"And I can ask my husband as well," Rebecca chimed in. "Eli would be only too happy to help restore The Quilting Barn."

"Is that what you call it?" Caleb asked. "The Quilting Barn?"

"Yes," Rebecca replied. "Isn't it a fine name?"

"It most definitely is," Caleb replied. He glanced out of the window at the barn. "The Quilting Barn," he murmured. "How very appropriate."

"So, when would you like David and Eli to come and help with the barn?" Lydia asked.

"The sooner the better," Caleb replied, his eyes still fixed on the barn, clearly visible through the window.

"I have to get home anyway," Rebecca said, "so I'll ask Eli to come over and to bring David with him."

"It will take a few days," Caleb said. "I hope that won't keep them from their own work."

"There isn't a lot for Eli to do on the farm during the winter," Rebecca replied. "And I'm sure David will feel the same way, so they will be here as soon as they can."

"Thank you," Caleb said. "You are very kind."

"Well, I would like to do whatever I can to get The Quilting Barn up and running again," Rebecca smiled. "It's such a major part of our lives."

"May we do anything else to help?" Lydia asked.

"I have a request," Caleb said.

"What is it?" Candace asked.

"My request is that you don't come into the barn until work on it is complete," Caleb answered.

"But I would naturally like to take a look at how the work is progressing," Candace protested.

"I will do that," Ruby said, entering the room. "Caleb has discussed the project with me, and it would be best if we left him and the other men to do their job. Don't worry, I can stop by and check on things every once in a while."

"Alright, if you insist," Candace said with a shrug.

"That Caleb Raber is such a fine young man," Ruby said later, as she and Candace prepared lunch for the men working on the barn roof.

"Well, he did an excellent job with my quilts," Candace grudgingly admitted, "and thanks to the quilts being moved, we discovered the damp back of the closet so that we could move the quilts to a better place and thus spare them any further damage."

"I feel like the Lord has sent him here," Ruby mused.

"Now, *Mamm*, let's not get carried away," Candace said sharply.

"Do you know that after the barn repairs are done, he has volunteered to help with any repairs of properties in the village damaged by the snow and rain?" Ruby announced reverently.

"Shouldn't he be getting back to Fair View?" Candace queried. "It's strange that he doesn't seem to want to resume his journey."

"Maybe he has a very good reason for staying on," Ruby remarked, giving Candace a significant look.

"I honestly couldn't guess what that reason could possibly be," Candace replied. "Maybe I should remind him that he's only here because he was on a bus that left him behind, and that he should remember he was bound for home."

"Right now, I'm making him some of his favorite stew," Ruby said, ignoring Candace's sharp tone. "Our Caleb loves it."

"*Our* Caleb? Is that what he is now?" Candace asked impatiently.

"Oh, my dear Candace, in the short time that he has been living with us, Caleb has become such a part of the family. He helps your *daed* too. So much. And we are ever so grateful."

"*Mamm*, I get the feeling that there's more to Caleb than meets the eye. He's hiding something," Candace remarked.

"Hush dear, he might hear you, and you wouldn't want him to be hurt after all he is doing, now would you?" Ruby said.

"Caleb appears to be guilty about something," Candace commented. "I don't know why, but that's the feeling I get. And what's more, he seems to be trying very hard to make up for whatever it is that he is guilty about."

"Why would you say something like that?" Ruby asked.

"Because he never stops trying to do things to help out," Candace answered.

"Maybe he's just a very good and helpful person," Ruby declared. "And I do hope you will see that one day."

"Miss Ruby," Caleb called from the porch, interrupting their conversation, "please, would you bring Candace out to the barn?"

Candace heard him and turned pink. The tone of his voice indicated that he was excited about something, and that the something was for her. She shook her head. She didn't want to be at all indebted to Caleb. They barely knew anything at all about him, and it disturbed Candace that Ruby was so ready to place all her trust in him.

"Candace," Ruby said, her voice tremulous with excitement. "Caleb, David and Eli have been working hard on repairing the barn, and they would like you to see what they've done. Well, Caleb would. David and Eli have left already."

"I can take a look later," Candace replied.

"No, dear child, you must come now!" Ruby insisted. "We are all so eager to show it to you."

Candace shrugged her shoulders. "Alright then," she sighed. "I'll come along."

Moments later, she was standing speechless inside the barn, her palms flying to her cheeks as her mouth fell open in wonder. "Oh my!" she exclaimed. "I had no idea…"

"It was meant to be a surprise," Caleb said, "and that's why we didn't want you to take a look while the work was going on."

"Candace, my dear," Ruby said, "look at the new closet! Isn't it perfect? And done so quickly too!"

"Oh my!" Candace repeated, holding her breath as she gazed at the new closet that Caleb had erected in place of the old one.

"I used the wood because it was good, but I reinforced the back rather than building the closet against the wall," Caleb said proudly. "Do you like it?"

"It's too much!" Candace said.

"Too much?" Ruby echoed. *"Too much? What are you saying, Candace?"*

"I mean, you shouldn't have gone to all this trouble, Caleb," Candace declared, looking up at Caleb. "That's what I mean when I say it's too much."

"But I wanted to do this for you, Candace," Caleb said. "To make up for…"

"Caleb, you made up for the quilts. You restored them. You didn't have to do all this as well," Candace interrupted him.

"Well, I think it's a very nice gesture," Ruby cut in. "And I want to say thank you, Caleb, from all of us."

***

"Now I feel obligated to him somehow," Candace admitted to Rebecca and Lydia.

"Eli said he accepted his and David's help with the roof, but he made the closet on his own," Rebecca said.

"And it's huge, and remarkably well finished, given the time frame he had to work on it," Lydia declared, her eyebrows raised in wonder.

"All our quilts will fit in nicely and be safe from the damp," Rebecca added.

Lydia was running her hand over the closet. "This is such a beautiful gesture."

"Why are you all so impressed with Caleb?" Candace burst out. "He's obviously doing all this for a reason. He's hiding something!"

***

"I've been hiding something," Caleb admitted later, looking down at his plate, shamefaced.

Candace looked up in slight shock, surprised to hear her words from the afternoon repeated by Caleb.

"I have been wondering all this time how I would tell you good people. But know this, I didn't mean to deceive you all. I just couldn't find a way to tell you the truth about myself."

Candace's knife and fork clattered onto her plate and her eyes flashed. "I knew it!" she said triumphantly.

"I overheard you speaking to Rebecca and Lydia," Caleb said, meeting her eye.

Candace turned red. "Look, Caleb, I'm sorry, but I can't help but wonder why you're still here in Crescent Creek when you only stopped by to take temporary shelter. And you have been working non-stop as if your life depended on it—doing chores, repairing the barn and building that incredible closet in such a short span of ten days or so. I would wake and hear you working at night and wondered if you slept at all. I also wondered what it was that was causing you so much guilt that you felt you had to compensate for something you did. It couldn't just be the quilts, because you had them back in perfect shape a while ago. So what…?"

"I ran away from Fair View some years ago," Caleb said, taking a deep breath. "And I lived with my aunt and uncle in Miller's Gap. Then, recently, I heard that my *mamm* was ailing, so I decided it was time I paid my family a visit and…"

"Why did you run away?" Candace asked. "Did you commit a crime?"

"We were having financial problems, and my *mamm* had started a baking business. She had a stall by our house, and few people knew about it. So, I knew I had to do something to help her out."

"What did you do?" Candace asked, her face tense.

"I had heard about the power of the Internet and "social media" while I was on Rumspringa, so I went to one of my Englischer friends and umm… asked for the loan of… his umm… laptop."

"What! Oh no!" Ruby exclaimed, but Candace's features relaxed a little.

"All I did was use skills that I had learned during Rumspringa to set up a social media page for my *mamm*… and it worked! Englischers from several towns came by to sample *Raber's Bakes*. My *mamm*, through her hard work, was able to pull our family out of debt. But she found the laptop in my room, and being the honest woman she is, took the matter to the Bishops and requested them to pardon me. But they told her I had transgressed and would have to be shunned. I was afraid and ran away from Fair View."

"You had a laptop in your room?" Ruby queried. "What is that? Some kind of device?"

"It's a computer, *Mamm*," Candace said. "But smaller."

"And the Internet is the world's window to every kind of sin, our Bishops said," Caleb added. "They didn't understand that I was just trying to help my *mamm's* new business venture in the only way that I knew would be truly effective." He shrugged. "We had tried simple handwritten leaflets and signs tacked to the trees in the village, but they didn't draw as much of a crowd as our social media ads did. My Englischer friend knows a thing or two about designing advertisements and such, and he was generous enough to help me out."

"And that's why you were going to be shunned?" Candace asked. "I see that what you did definitely goes against our beliefs, but perhaps they could have let you off with a public apology."

"Well," Caleb said, "I couldn't live with the shame of it all, and so I left and didn't go back. That is, until my attempt a few weeks ago."

"Perhaps it was God's will that the bus left you behind," Ruby said comfortingly.

Caleb shook his head, his eyes fixed on the plate before him. "I'm afraid that's the second part of my confession. I told a lie. The bus didn't leave me behind. It was I that asked the bus to stop and then got off and ran and ran, until by God's grace I found your barn."

"But you do want to go back and be reunited with your family, don't you?" Candace asked.

"I want to see my *mamm*," Caleb replied. "I heard she was unwell, and then I heard she was better. But whatever her state of health, I want to put the past behind and go back to my family, except that I don't have the courage to face the bishops and take whatever punishment is meted out to me." He clenched his fists as he fought his emotions. "For a long time, I was angry with my *mamm*. You see, I had borrowed the laptop with the sole purpose of helping her out, and I was going to return it. But she went to the Bishops to tell them about it, purely because she felt it was the right thing for her to do, and never considering what it would do to me."

"Your *mamm* is an honorable woman," Ruby said. "So you must never resent her for what she did."

"And I applaud you for what you did for her," Candace declared. "Though the means used were against our rules and way of life, your motivations were honorable too. So first of all, Caleb, you need to forgive yourself, and then you need to return to Fair View to reunite with your family and explain your heart to the Bishops. I'm sure they will forgive you too."

"I've never been able to look at a laptop, or indeed any modern technology, ever again," Caleb replied. "So I haven't transgressed before or since that event. Perhaps I ought to go back and tell the Bishops that."

"And we will come with you," Candace said. "For moral support."

"Or to make sure that I indeed go back home?" Caleb laughed. "I don't blame you all. I have overstayed my welcome, for sure, and I am now making inquiries in the village for a place to stay where I can do chores to pay for my keep."

"But shouldn't you go home, son?" Ruby ventured.

"As soon as I'm ready and have got up the courage, I most certainly will," Caleb replied.

"In that case," Ruby said, "where better to stay than right here where you are at home?"

Caleb glanced uncertainly at Candace and then turned back to her mother. "Are you certain, Miss Ruby?" he asked.

"I am, Caleb," Ruby replied.

Candace looked uncomfortable. She got up and went to fetch some more bread and set it on the table. Then, clearing her throat, she said, "Caleb, I want to thank you, from the bottom of my heart, for building that beautiful closet for the barn… and for being so honest with us right now. And if there's anything else that you're concealing from us, I hope you will let us know."

CHAPTER FOUR

Caleb took Ruby's list and cycled down to the mercantile with Candace's words echoing in his head. *"If there's anything else that you're concealing from us, I hope you will let us know,"* she had said, and Caleb hadn't been able to meet her gaze when she spoke the words. They had finished the meal in silence, broken only when Amos joined them, apologizing for being late because he had gone to visit his mother.

"There are some relationships that we must never take for granted or let go of," Amos had said when Caleb had told him the truth about himself. "I sometimes have to miss having a meal with my wife and children because duty calls me to my *mamm's* side when she is unwell or just needs to see me. So son, don't let your pride get in the way, or even your consternations. Just go and see your *mamm.*"

The Shrocks were such good people, Caleb mused, as he pedaled towards the mercantile. And Candace, she didn't seem to be aware of just how big an impression she was making on people—especially on him. Her large blue eyes had him mesmerized from the beginning, and all he wanted was to win her approval any way that he could. How glad he was that she had finally admitted that she was happy about the closet. He had put in his best work on it and done with minimal sleep so that he could finish it as quickly as he had managed to.

"Caleb!" he heard Rebecca call out.

"*Wie bisht du?*" Eli asked from her side.

"Hello, Rebecca. I am well, thanks, Eli," Caleb replied to his new friends. If only Candace would be as accepting of him as Rebecca, Eli, Lydia and David were. If only she would smile at him.

"I'm here to pick up some groceries for Miss Ruby," Caleb explained.

"You are such a big help to the Shrocks," Rebecca remarked. "They must be so happy with all that you do for them."

"They do a lot for me, too," Caleb replied. "Their generosity in allowing me to stay with them indefinitely while I work out some things that I need to is something I will ever be grateful for."

"That's what our community is all about. We are all there for each other," Eli said.

"Rebecca," Caleb ventured, when they were inside the store, "what gift could I give Miss Ruby, Mister Amos and Candace?"

"You repaired the barn and built Candace the most incredible closet," Rebecca replied. "But I think I know what she would like—a hand-painted sign for the barn."

"You mean a sign that says The Quilting Barn?" Caleb asked.

Rebecca nodded.

Caleb shrugged. "I could make a sign for sure, but that's not a big gift at all."

Rebecca patted Caleb on his arm. "I'm sure you'll think of something appropriate," she said.

"And for Miss Ruby and Mister Amos?" Caleb queried.

Rebecca laughed. "You know what the greatest gift would be that you could give them? Find Candace a suitable groom. Their greatest desire is to see her married and settled before she turns twenty-one."

Caleb raised his eyebrows. "Oh, is that so!"

"I am just speaking light-heartedly, but it's a serious issue for them. Especially since I am married and Lydia is courting," Rebecca declared.

"I see," Caleb murmured.

"Alright then, we'll see you around," Eli said, as he and Rebecca prepared to leave with their purchases. "I have to go to a barn raising."

"May I come too?" Caleb asked. "After I drop these groceries off at the Shrocks' house?"

"Of course," Eli replied. "The more, the merrier."

"Where's Caleb gone now?" Candace asked Ruby as the two women prepared the afternoon meal together.

"He said he was going for a barn raising with Eli," Ruby replied.

"He appears to be stalling again," Candace remarked. "He should be making plans to go to his home village and get his life back on track, don't you think?"

"Or maybe he's getting his life on track right here," Ruby said, "and will then visit his village."

"I don't see how he's getting his life on track by attending barn raisings and helping out with chores," Candace murmured.

"How's the quilting coming along?" Ruby asked, changing the subject.

Candace brightened up. "I'm eagerly looking forward to opening up The Quilting Barn to customers in a few months, when we have enough quilts to display," she replied.

"You need to leave some time free to attend Sings and Frolics," Ruby said matter-of-factly, "or you will never be married before you're twenty-one."

"Oh *Mamm*, not the marriage talk again!" Candace remarked impatiently.

"Candace, my dear, you know how I worry. All your siblings are settled, and so are your friends. Even Lydia and David have set a date for next fall," Ruby said.

"They have?" Candace queried. "I didn't know. Lydia didn't say anything to me."

"She probably doesn't want you to feel bad that you're still single and no closer to courting or becoming engaged than you were at the beginning of this year," Ruby said with a shrug.

Candace made a face, furiously rolling pastry all the while. She knew that her mother was right about Lydia's motives for not telling her about her upcoming wedding. And it hurt. She wished she had met someone appropriate and was courting.

Well, she had met someone, but he wasn't exactly appropriate. For one thing, he wasn't from her village and for another, he hadn't got his life on track. Plus, she wasn't quite sure how exactly she felt about him—whether she just felt a strange fascination for a stranger who had landed up in her barn one snowy night, or was developing some deeper feelings for the mystery man who had charmed her family and friends with his readiness to help and be a part of anything and everything that took place in Crescent Creek.

She thought of the closet he had built for her and the care with which he had called her out to the barn to show it to her. He was a good man, was Caleb, if a little confused by life at times. Or was he being a little… cowardly? How did she feel about a man who was so good in so many ways, but lacked the courage to face the consequences of his actions, she wondered.

"We need to urge him to go to his village," Candace said suddenly.

"Who?" Ruby asked. "We were talking about you just now, my child."

"Caleb," Candace replied. "He must go home and get his life back on track."

"I agree. Let's talk to him again," Ruby said.

"It's vital that he not be a coward and that he be courageous. It's important, you know, *Mamm*," Candace declared earnestly.

Ruby left her place by the oven and came to stand next to her daughter, peering anxiously into her face.

"This concern for Caleb, this desire to see him as a courageous person, could it be because…?" Ruby began.

"*Mamm*!" Candace exclaimed. "What are you implying?"

"Just wondering, my dear, just wondering," Ruby replied, and there was a lilt in her voice. "If you think that it's important that Caleb go back home, then I will urge him with everything I've got, and so will your *daed*. Oh, my dear child, I know what you mean, and you don't have to spell it out just yet, but I've seen it in your eyes, and in his as well—which is why I've encouraged him to stay on."

Candace almost dropped the pie that she was taking out of the oven.

"What!" she exclaimed. "What are you talking about, *Mamm*? What have you seen in my eyes, or in his?"

"That look of realization, my dear. Or perhaps you could call it a look of wonder. Of complete surprise at the way in which you both have met. It's a strange and wondrous way, to be sure. But it's the Lord's way. As for the look in

Caleb's eyes… Oh, Candace, how much he wants to please you, to win your approval and to make you happy. That seems to be his life's mission."

"It's only because of the quilts," Candace said with a careless shrug, though her heart beat faster.

"The quilts may have been the beginning, but the barn, and the closet… My dear, that was just his heart trying to please you. You can be sure of it."

"Oh my!" Candace said, setting the pie down on the table. "I honestly don't want to feel indebted to anyone, least of all Caleb," she said. "I've said this before."

"He is drawn to you, Candace, I can tell," Ruby declared emphatically.

"*Mamm*, please don't say anymore," Candace said. "Because it will only make things very awkward between Caleb and me."

"My lips are sealed," Ruby said with a wink and a smile. "But only for now!"

CHAPTER FIVE

"You've been behaving mysteriously," Candace observed, looking at Lydia over the quilt she was working on. "You and Rebecca, both."

"Really?" Lydia murmured. "I honestly don't think I've been behaving any differently from the way I normally do."

"It's about the fact that you've fixed a date with David and haven't told me, isn't it?" Candace said.

"David and I have fixed a date, and I was going to tell you, Candace," Lydia said. "But I was just looking for the right moment."

"But Rebecca knows, doesn't she?" Candace queried.

"She does," Lydia replied. "I won't lie to you. But we both didn't know how to tell you. You see…"

"It's because I'm not engaged, or courting or have anyone in sight yet…?" Candace said bitterly.

"You're making it sound like we are being mean to you, and nothing could be further from the truth," Lydia replied. "We care about you,

Candace. And anyway, though I don't want to tell you, because it is supposed to be a secret, Rebecca and I have been behaving mysteriously because Caleb has asked us to help him plan something. It's a surprise… for you."

"What?" Candace faltered, dropping her quilt.

"Caleb really wants to help you, and us, with The Quilting Barn, so he has a plan which he wants to surprise you with," Lydia said.

"And what is this plan?" Candace asked. "Which you are hiding from me?"

"Candace," Lydia said. "This is for you. It's not a bad thing. It's a good plan, believe me."

"What is it, Lydia?" Candace asked. "I thought Caleb had already given me a surprise with the repaired barn, the closet and then the very elaborate sign for The Quilting Barn."

"Candace, Caleb truly cares about you," Lydia whispered. "So much so that he will go to any lengths to make you happy."

"What is the surprise?" Candace asked stubbornly.

"You'll get to know very soon," Lydia reassured her.

Just then, there was a knocking on the barn door. Lydia jumped up and threw the door open.

Outside stood a horde of people, with Caleb right in front of them.

"So this is it," Caleb said. "The Quilting Barn—the only one of its kind in the village of Crescent Creek."

Candace jumped up and exclaimed in surprise, and Rebecca sprang out from the crowd and hurried to her side.

"Please, Candace, just smile and be happy," she whispered. "Caleb has brought a lot of prospective customers to see your quilts... and ours."

"But we don't have enough, and besides, this is our enterprise, and I never asked him to do any of this," Candace whispered back. Outwardly she smiled at the crowd as Rebecca and Lydia guided people in and showed them the quilts that they had.

"So these quilts will give you an idea of what you can have custom-made by this team of extremely talented quilters," Caleb said. "Look, here's a quilt made for a bride-to-be, and there's one for a couple about to celebrate their Silver Wedding Anniversary."

People swarmed all over the barn, and by the end of a couple of hours, Candace, Lydia and Rebecca had more orders for quilts than they knew what to do with.

"I know it was very kind of you, and a novel idea indeed," Candace said to Caleb later in her kitchen, "but how will we meet these orders in a reasonable enough time frame while still maintaining the quality we want to be known for?"

"I was only trying to help," Caleb replied.

"Like you tried to help your *mamm*, using the Internet which we regard as sinful?" Candace shot back, the words out before she could stop them.

"Candace, my child, aren't you being harsh?" Ruby said, trying to restrain her daughter from saying anything further.

"Harsh? *Mamm*, what's harsh is that Caleb took our business venture into his hands without consulting me. He took Rebecca and Lydia into his confidence, saying he wanted to surprise me. Still, I am beginning to wonder if it wasn't merely to indulge some whim of his."

"Do you think this was a whim, Candace?" Caleb asked quietly, his face very white and his jaw tense.

"I am just wondering, Caleb, about your motivations. This is my venture, and I should have been consulted about any methods you chose to publicize it," Candace replied.

"As I mentioned several times before, Candace, it was meant to be a surprise," Caleb said.

"Surprises are meant for birthdays or other occasions, Caleb," Candace retorted. "But they are hardly appropriate when it's the question of a serious business venture… and when you keep the main business partner out of the plan and shock her with a stream of orders that she barely knows how to fulfill!"

Caleb gave Candace a strange look and shook his head. Then he turned to Ruby.

"Miss Ruby," he said, "I want to thank you and Mister Amos for putting me up for so long. But the time has come for me to move out."

He turned on his heel and strode away, his shoulders squared and his mouth set in a thin, hard line.

CHAPTER SIX

"I think you dealt rather unfairly with Caleb," Rebecca said.

"What about the way you and Lydia dealt with me? Keeping secrets from me?" Candace cried.

"Don't you understand anything at all, Candace? Why are you being so blind?" Lydia said. "Caleb is in love with you. And I am certain that you're in love with him. He doesn't have the courage or probably can't find the words in which to tell you about his feelings, so he does things like this—surprising you in ways that he thinks will bring you joy."

"How are you so certain, as you say, that I have feelings for Caleb?" Candace asked.

"Because the whole village knows and sees, except you," Rebecca declared.

"And with all due respect, Candace," Rebecca replied, "The Quilting Barn is supposed to belong to all of us. Now I know that the barn is your family's, but the venture is equally yours, mine, and Lydia's... and the other women who join us from time to time to quilt together. So please don't behave as if it's only yours and that you can't handle all the orders. Lydia and I sat down with the orders, and we have spread them across all of us who quilt together. Guess what? When we all work together, we can meet these orders… and more."

"It would seem that you are always looking for something to be angry with Caleb about," Lydia added. "And believe me, it took me a while to discern the reason, but I see it all too clearly now. You wish that he would declare his feelings for you, but just as he doesn't have the courage to go back home and face his elders and family, he obviously doesn't have enough courage to tell you how he feels. And perhaps that makes you angry."

***

Candace left the barn and walked over to the house. Snowflakes swirled around her, melting on her *kaap* and gown and dotting the cape across her shoulders. The winter chill pierced her heart and lay like a block of ice within her.

It had been two weeks since Caleb had left, and she missed him. She also realized that Lydia was right. She wished that Caleb would tell her how he felt in words, rather than give her surprises or try to be a part of her village in order to fit into her world.

She stopped midway in her reflections and realized that Caleb must feel very deeply for her if he did all he could to fit into her life and her world. She had thought it was for his own convenience, and because he wanted to put off returning home. Now, however, she realized while that might have been one of his motivations for doing what he did, he also did it because of his feelings for her.

She wiped a tear off her cheek. She had lost an opportunity to be with someone who truly cared about her, and now she would perhaps end up living her life all alone, sitting in her Quilting Barn making quilts while her friends went on to have families of their own and lives rich with love and meaning.

"Candace, my child," Ruby said, calling to her daughter from the front door, "come inside and eat something. You look so lost that it breaks my heart."

Reluctantly Candace went indoors, hanging her head and unwilling to meet her parents' eyes.

"Candace," Amos said, "perhaps your *mamm* and I can take the buggy over to Fair View village to visit Caleb and his family and see how they are doing. I know you must be concerned for his welfare, as are we."

"You could come with us if you like," Ruby added.

"*Mamm, Daed*, thank you… but I deserve this," Candace said tearfully. "I wasn't very fair to Caleb, as my friends pointed out, and I don't deserve his friendship. He tried very hard to do things that he thought would make me happy, and I was ungrateful. So, if you want to visit Fair View and check on Caleb, please do it for him and not for me, because I really don't deserve any kindness at this point."

"Everyone deserves grace and forgiveness," Amos said. "And so do you. You are but a child, Candace, and you made a mistake. I'm sure Caleb has forgiven you already."

"I only hope he has gone to be with his family and hasn't gone anywhere else where he might be alone," Candace said, surprising herself with her own anxiety over Caleb's safety and wellbeing.

The next morning, she rushed through her chores, eager to get to the barn and find solace in the new quilt she was creating. While she was at work, the pain over Caleb became a dull ache. It was when she went back to the house and sat at the table looking at the chair he had occupied until two weeks ago, and remembered the many times she had treated him unkindly, that the ache became a searing pain. She hoped that Rebecca, Lydia and the other women would join her soon, so that the barn would reverberate with laughter and conversation, even if she wasn't a wholehearted participant.

As if in answer to her silent wishes, the barn door creaked open.

"*Gute mariye!*" Candace called over her shoulder, bowed over her work, and infusing more cheer into her voice than she actually felt.

When she didn't get a reply from Rebecca, Lydia or any of the others, Candace turned around and then jumped up from her chair.

"Caleb!" she exclaimed.

"Candace," Caleb murmured, his eyes roving over her face, as if he were looking for something. They lingered over her eyes, and then, as they locked onto them, Caleb seemed reassured and moved closer to her.

"What… brings you back?" Candace asked, her voice catching in her throat. "I'm sorry…"

"You're sorry I'm back?" Caleb asked, drawing back briefly.

"No," Candace said quickly. "I'm sorry if I was hurtful. And ungrateful."

"Candace, it is I who have returned to seek your forgiveness," Caleb said.

"What for?" Candace asked.

"For not being completely honest with you," Caleb replied. "Remember when I told you the truth about my past, and you asked me if there was anything else that I was hiding from you all?"

Candace said nothing. She just nodded silently.

"Well," Caleb said. "I have been hiding something very important from you, Candace."

Candace's eyes were filled with trepidation as Caleb moved even closer and reached out to place the tip of his finger on her cheek.

"I have been so very much in love with you for ever so long, Candace," Caleb whispered, "but I couldn't find the courage to tell you."

Candace drew in her breath sharply and held it as Caleb stroked her cheek and gazed into her eyes, whispering things she had wanted to hear from his lips for ever so long.

"Oh, Caleb," Candace whispered back. "I was angry with you for doing all those things for me, because I honestly just wanted you to tell me…"

"That I love you?" Caleb completed her sentence. "Well, I am going to tell you now, over and over, and then for the rest of our lives… if you will forgive me for my foolishness and consider spending the rest of your life with me."

"What are you saying?" Candace asked, her heart beginning to pound. She felt almost dizzy.

"Perhaps I should repaint the cow byre and mend the fence in the pigsty," Caleb replied, his face breaking into a smile. "I'm just joking. I realized what I was doing and what I ought to be doing. My *mamm* made me see sense."

"Your *mamm*?" Candace asked eagerly. "Did you go back home to your family?"

"I did," Caleb answered. "And I made a full confession to our Bishops and was forgiven by our village Community. But I also bid a final farewell to Fair View."

"You did? Why?" Candace asked.

"Because not only have I fallen in love with you, Candace, but also with Crescent Creek and the people here. I want to live here, close to you until the day when you say yes to my question."

"What is the question?" Candace asked.

"Candace Shrock," Caleb said, "will you let me spend the rest of my life, and yours, doing things that surprise you and make you happy?"

"Caleb," Candace said, with a smile, "you're doing it again."

"You're right," Caleb said, swallowing, "I'm terrified at this moment, but I'm going to be brave and say it out loud. Candace Shrock, will you marry me?"

Candace didn't take her eyes from his. She reached up to grasp his hand as he continued to stroke her cheek. This was proving to be too much emotion for her to handle, and she wondered if she would just faint from the intensity of it all.

"Caleb Raber, I will, but only if you promise to keep surprising me," she replied.

"And now come inside and meet my *mamm* and *daed*," Caleb smiled. "They can't wait to get to know you."

"Your *mamm* and *daed* are here?" Candace asked. "In the house?"

"Yes," Caleb answered. "My *mamm* insisted I come back and tell you how I feel. And my *daed* too."

"I can't wait to meet them," Candace said, taking Caleb's hand.

And together, they turned towards the house, both eager to embrace and love and new surprises life had in store for them.

The End

Please Check out My Other Works

By checking out the link below

http://cleanromancepublishing.com/rbauth

Thank You

Many thanks for taking the time to buy and read through this book.

It means lots to be supported by SPECIAL readers like YOU.

Hope you enjoyed the book; please support my writing by leaving an honest review to assist other readers.

.

With Regards,

Ruth Bawell